Get Reading! B

New School: Day One

Boston, Massachusetts

ELA

This is Rita.

She's from Mexico, but she lives in Texas now. She lives in a large city with her mother. There are many young people in the **neighborhood**, but Rita doesn't know any of them.

It's her first day at her new school. She's a little bit scared and **nervous**! Everything is so different now!

nervous

Rita looks at her mother. "I'm so nervous," she says.

"I know," her mother says. "But you're strong. Remember when you were a little girl? What did we used to say?"

Rita smiles. She remembers. She puts her hands on her hips and says, "I can do it! I am Super Rita!"

Rita and her mother laugh. Then, they wave good-bye and Rita walks to school smiling.

Rita's mother used to call her "Super Rita." She called her that many years ago.

Rita arrives at her new school. It's so big and different from her old school. There are many classrooms and hallways. The biggest difference is all the new faces!

Rita gets nervous. Then, she says, "It's OK. I can do it. I just have to find the office. Now where is it?" She looks around and starts walking down the hallway.

Rita soon finds the office. The school secretary is standing behind a counter. "Good morning!" she says.

Rita **takes a deep breath**. "Hello. I'm Rita Flores. It's my first day. Where should I go?"

"Welcome, Rita!" says the secretary. She looks at her computer. She gives Rita some papers and a **map**. "You're in class 11A, room 18," she explains. "Just follow the map!"

Rita has to move quickly. Class starts in five minutes! She gets nervous. Then, she stops and takes a deep breath. "I can do it!" she thinks.

Students **rush** by. One boy almost hits Rita! He smiles and says, "Sorry!" Then, he rushes away.

Rita checks her map. "OK. There's the music room, and there's room 18. So I **go straight**, then left at the gym."

Rita walks down the hallway. She sees a big room. It's the gym! "I did it!" she thinks.

She looks inside and gets excited. Basketball! She loves basketball! "I can join the team!" she thinks. She waves "hello" to the gym teacher. Then, she remembers. "Basketball later," she tells herself. "First, my class. I can't **be late** on my first day!"

Rita looks at her map again. "OK, room 18. Where are you?" she says. There are many doors in the hallway. She looks carefully. "There's room 15. I must be close!"

Rita looks again. She sees room 16, then room 17, and... there it is! room 18! Rita is so happy that she forgets to be nervous. "I did it!" she says.

KNOW IT ALL

Trying something new? Think of something happy or funny. It can make you forget about being nervous or scared.

Rita looks into the room. There are a lot of students! They're all talking and laughing together. They're all friends. And Rita doesn't know anyone!

She gets nervous again. Then, she thinks about her mother's words. "I can do it! I'm Super Rita," she says. It makes her laugh. She takes a deep breath and walks into the room.

Rita walks up to the teacher and says, "Hi. I'm Rita Flores. Today is my first day."

"Good morning, Rita," says the teacher. "Welcome! Please **take a seat**."

Rita finds a desk and sits down. She puts the map by her bag. She puts her pencil and notebook on her desk. She's ready to write down any **important** information.

"I'm Mr. Curran," says the teacher. He begins talking about school. He talks about classes, activities, and **homework**. Rita writes it all down.

Soon it's lunchtime. The students start to leave. As they walk past, Mr. Curran says, "Don't forget! Basketball **practice** is on Monday!"

"Great!" thinks Rita. "I'll go to that!" She writes the information in her notebook.

Rita finishes writing. She puts her notebook into her bag and walks to the door.

"OK. So, now where's the cafeteria?" she says. "I need my map!" She looks in her bag. It's not there! She looks around. It's not on her desk or on the floor. "Oh no!" she says. "Where's my map?"

Rita walks out of the classroom. She looks up and down the hallway. It's nearly empty. There are just a few students.

"OK. There's the music room, and there's the science room," she says. "But where's the cafeteria?"

She turns left down one hallway. She turns right down another. There's no cafeteria. Rita is lost.

Rita is lost. She can't find the cafeteria.

"What am I going to do?" thinks Rita. Then she sees a girl. "OK, Super Rita. You can do it!" she thinks. She takes a deep breath and walks over. "Hi," she says. "It's my first day. Where's the cafeteria?"

The girl smiles. She shows Rita a paper. It's a map! "I dont know. Please use my map," the girl says. "I'm Amira. It's my first day, too. I'm so nervous! I don't know anyone."

Rita smiles back. "That's not true," she says. "You know me! I'm Rita. Let's find the cafeteria together, OK?"

The girls walk with the map. Soon they find the cafeteria. "We did it!" says Amira happily.

"Yes, we did!" says Rita. "Not bad for day one at our new school!"

neighborhood the area in which you live

nervous worried and a little afraid about something

take a deep breath to breathe in very slowly and take in a lot of air, often done to relax

map a drawing of a place that shows you where to go

rush to move very quickly

go straight to go forward in a line

be late to show up after the time you should be somewhere

take a seat to sit down

important needed or of value

homework school work that is to be done at home

practice the action of doing something again and again to get better at it